vorsexual

enochisms

vorsexual enochisms

A collection of lyric prose

Authored by

lebeyt.

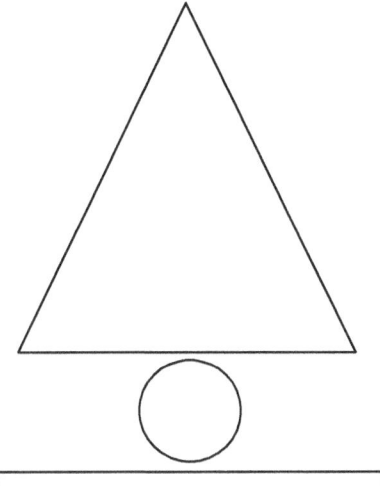

Dancehall University Books

ISBN-13: 978-0-692-90264-6
Printed in the United States of America

dedication

my tinish.

opening my center black hole elixir
wetting.

table of contents

(source of the nile

((morning

(((afternoon

((((my star

spiral

love perceptions

appreciate

poa

la

_____

bad dreams

<u>im confessing</u>

<u>newness</u>

<u>catching feelins</u>

<u>perspectives</u>

<u>shifting</u>

_____

so sweet

☾ 🔺🔻 lyrics

☾☾ 🔺🔻 king b

☾☾☾ 🔺🔻 grateful

☾☾☾☾ 🔺🔻 100 choices

divine that i am

 visualization

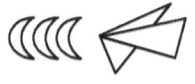 remembering

 if it aint you

most high guide

my conscious

 love's hostage

 jah

 uncertain

 shakey investments

mpersonate   ◯

☾ ◯   synchronized

☾☾ ◯   no one night stand

☾☾☾ ◯   expectations

author's note

Vorsexual-Enochisms is a journey through the heights of the divine feminine intersecting with the lows of the alleged mortal female condition. For centuries women have been chastised to believe that suppressing their sexual centers would result in a higher-mind. Consequently it is through the activation of those energies that open a vortex that most easily links humanity with the subconscious all knowing.

I've come to see my spiritual journey as a kind of path to nirvana like the Buddha but at the astral level as described in the *Lost Book of Enoch* all with the divine feminine at the center. Vorsexual-Enochisms translates those nostalgic vibrations from a contemporary voice you might expect from a LA native and distant ancestor of the Abyssinian who penned the aforementioned *lost book*. A Moses if you will, born abroad up-stream along the Nile yet raised downstream possessing a direct link to the ancient mystics of lore.

It is often asserted; *if you ever want to know the universe, you must look within.* And when are you most concentrated on within? Is it not at that point of deepest orgasm? Is it not at this moment that even new life must conceive?

preface

...I soon found myself in the ancient Valley of the Great Rift listening to the wind, feeling the stars, interfacing with the materialization of the world within. Was it my location on the equatorial line, the soil of my ancestors beneath my feet? Were the pyramids nearby sending signals? Orion's belt above my head yet aligned at Giza. My perspective is making me blind. Sirius was my guide. My electrodes plugged in with my ancient environment. The energy flowing from the Nile activated my internal receptors. Much has been lost at the hands of self-appointed info-distributors (I'm looking at you British Museum). But some knowledge can never be lost, like Enoch. Be in the right place at the right time on the right vibes and realize the stream is never-ending. It was a cold war. 2.5 years. Words were my water. All I needed. Only one option. Survive to read it. There ain't no rules. No ref.

No do over's just forward with all the fractures and with all the laughter cause…spiritual war ain't fair.

☾ source of the nile

Source of the Nile begins in me. Reflecting

who I was and who I thought I'd be.

Elevations

Holistic understandings ready for lifting, no more
bending

For someone who ain't see that unity is just the

beginning.

Opportunistic questions. No listening
Love circumstances. Ego weakening

Not knowing what to love and what to hate about
me. Feminine tendencies.

Love undermining-hiding the man
      underneath. Childlike.
Never rising above deficiencies.
           Can't stand light, wishing to hold me
hostage, sexually chastised
Thinking emotional verbiage
      can keep me waiting
         Hoping for alleged reunification
              Manipulation
Wishing we could be. When we can't. Punctuations
What you know about haters in your bed?
Tryna fuck up your medz
          The head beyond-belief
Soaring temporarily
Distractions from life's purpose

Necessities

       manifestations

       cosmic blessings

But they can't see or praise them cause they lack

       creativity

           pineal activation

Hating and debating spiteful maintaining

Looking for pride outside. Chest-puffin consumerist-

spending-slaving. No time for reallocations

               Prioritizing securing building

His upbringing seeping into the now

Imma stop though

        My energy fading

          Tryna raise-him

          When he change-hating

Weak conversations

               Getting worth falsely

Sex

Material

Social accepted understandings

                   TV

Can't see when I'm looking directly

Opening my center black-hole elixir-wetting

Revealing everything that is and ever was

               swirling and sweating

Star seeds planetary foundations

                Moon mixing sun-burning

                fire-birthing

                    then setting

magnetically drawn in and out through me

take advantage my king

sit at my feet

        let me

                go deep

((

Every morning I wake up here

I'm filled with a sense of peace

This is my favorite time of the day living in Et

      Birds burst out

          chirps bubbling from deep

Rising alone is a beautiful thing but waking up

      with your love could be ecstatic

Lovers get swept away easy if they release baggage

Love rides on the tails of sex flapping in the wind

The possibility of it actually touching you is there

      but slim

Sex is the vehicle love the destination

But it doesn't always lead there

so you gotta pay attention

When you arrive you know it you understand

      magnetism

Like spark plugs looking for its electrical-

      connections

Positive and negative fires burn

Loins yearn for its opposite and react

      Anticipations

Bodies join and rise beyond dimensions

 intense climax

Eyes closed conscious-dreams

star-floating heaven-touring

Been ready for them feelings after love-lost

10,000 miles & seven-years from what I thought

Free to explore social-misconceptions

Hurt & confused by loves-cost

The price of love is a broken-heart so my

        judgment's been-off

Looking with my eyes finding only weeds

Trying to choke the life and love out of me

Sexin wanting to re manifest the love I've seen

Left deplete giving more than I receive

                    Two negatives canceling

Till I realize sex is a funny thing

           Can lead to health and destruction

A vehicle for channeling

Heavenly communications. Ecclesiastic language

translations. Body jerking reflexes reactions.

Stroking and soothing cell-rejuvenations

Wu-wei. Effortless-action

afternoon

Opening chakras meridian aligning

When we're making love we are flying

consciously-climbing

He's on top rhyming making music & stayin on beat

Who eva said if you light you weak?

Maybe you are a product of your environment

you think ?

DNA changing with every second you sleep

Equatorial-regions African-living

So what happen to dem?

I can't help but keep thinking

Too much chat
no luck after chewing
Opposing the suns vitamin D
No-sleep Serotonin

No pineal activity pot-bellied
alcohol and sweets shrinking woods & capacities
Paying for sex legally
pill-poppin to get an erection
Molly, x & v's tryna make up for p's... the asian-african
Adolescent grown men, no accountability
Mamas defend behavior breaches-bleached
might as well be the enemy under-coverings
Skin is a thing you never know what's beneath
can hide war or peace

It's the light in the darkest parts I should seek

each human unique

Careful when opening

divinity happens in the silence underneath

So who said if you light

you can't work between the sheets?

Well then. Love opening me up to over-standings

climbing different dimensions

Seen a man who caught my attention-challenging

my perspective-formerly passing judgment

eyes begin to focus

pupil dilations

His light blinding

piercing outward thru me

African intentions speak silently to me

A language boundary free and I'm closing in

A righteous inspiration- spirits kindred

Flash back, caribbean - white-sands

you eva see rastafari tap dance?

kickin- back coonin, no repatriation, cash-flowing,

who's losing ? sex-touring

i'm asking it's whose delusion?

Then this one appears & he ain't faking nothing

Sweetness dripping. Love is the answer preaching

talking to my soul . let your light shine he beckons

breaking down my walls till my heart start

leaking

Soul reaching out from my sternum. He looking

thru me

Where you been when I was crying confused and
lying
Closed off-running from the truth
now I'm open
Divine timing

my star

60 degrees NE. Always with me
        Guiding silently
Ions raining
            seeding realities
Radiating thru the present and future me
                        Dualities
Former shyness diminishing
Trauma revealing underlying feelings
Emotional buildings ready for release
Skyscrapers falling yester-year's she evolving
Wanting more. Universe-calling

Searching for highness naturally

                                       Divine connections

No mediums

                        mixing and burning concoctions

No companions. earthly distraction. 3rd

dimensional dealings . Energetic sapping

Saturday nights No Sunday love mappings

Back where I began Alone pay my taxi to get

home

Fools luck trappings. Contracting without

reading lines   in between

Its ascensions I need metaphysically

Light permeating a goddess earthly dwelling

Soul snapping fingers impatiently

Looking deep hoping for a glimpse

Heavenly reflections in eyes
Above heads aura inspections
It's looking bleak. Eyes glazing from alcohol
and meat. Lips moving. Only discuss TV
My interest dimming
Past mistakes unveiling possibilities
For a reason. Everything. I'm learning
No more regretting reality bending
Figuring I can just stoop to meet
Entities locally. Low vibrating beings
Avoiding the higher me. Faking simplicity
Before I make my retreat
Remembering what I'm meant to be
Loving self physically
Floating spiritually

Emotions no longer take-lead
It's me my mission to explode esoterically
No more divisions. Clinging to 2nd and 3rd
dimensions. Forgetting source
No lightning infatuations

Charged electrically
There's more. Be open to receive
Particles condensing into all I need
Magnetized towards my center
      point
         Solar plexus
Black holes transmuting. Magic happening
from deep. Conception sparking then
breathing. Life force Divine redemption

Learning ancient lessons again, ascension

∇ 　spiral

Light years ahead. Ancient

Black holes and webs. Creation

Comets racing crashing then splitting in two

Conception

Focused on the truth

Source

Energizing galaxies. Consistently

Me shining bright. Twinkling

Giving thanks for light. Completing

Absorbing and releasing.

Magnetizing those adding to the energy I'm

emitting. Electrically

Happy just for living. Outshining
Thankfulness for existence. Letting my life be
the medium. Vision
Focusing on the source. Intuition
Remembering who I am and who I've been.
Connection. Never distant
Cus the currants move through me
And I get shocked. Electric lift in
Lights turn up to the 10th degree.
Exhibiting what I have received
Proving. Graciousness. All I need
Recollecting star wars. Galaxies
Ambitions At its height. The ultimate fight

competing just to shine-giving thanks for life.

Opportunity days. Soaking up rays.

Flickering. De-lighting just to charge.

Reappearing in the dark more bright

And despite Your thoughts. I'm free

Spiral rites

love perceptions

Lustful thoughts of you seeping through

        Meditations

brain

sex

herbs

repeat mind-projections

           no more wait-in

stiff digging with dat heat

Split-streams

          mean conduction

Waves float before they crash

Water falls

particle lessons

Your body on top of mine

Right now

tactile connection

Warming then steaming

Boiling over

releasing toxins

Energetic exchange

Body games. sensations

No cost

No love lost

No regret to save faces

No fights to keep faking

Chastising. Sacrificing. No-judgments

No more reason

No more social accepted prisons

        Fuck that flow resistance

Can't you see the implications

My love for you be racing

Flies below valleys boo

High above mountain-regions

Time-space-dimensions

Earthly speeches Verbatim

Cosmic elevations

Abundance

        No more wasting

Still you cold like ice cream

Watching truth thru blurred-vision

Loving me with restrictions

Hating my intuition

Forget myself for love maintaining

Me wanting more Yet nothing ever gaining

Dreaming we could flee to new galaxies

Saturn's ring

Different realms of understanding

Heart speaking Telepathically

Thankfulness for each other's

presence earthly

New seeds young trees

King & queen breeding

Distance makes it easy to listen

Geographically free from

Quote unquote love's conditions

Sex and lustful conversations

Pyramids and the sphinx

Ass up head down I make em come before

        release

Goddess realizing constellation gazing

Cells rejuvenating chakra approaching

Floating Conscious Endorphins

Body currents. electric

Magnetism

of all I need

        I attract it

And what I don't

It just leaves

        Like magic

           Bet that

appreciate

What you got when you see it don't waste it

Cus just in 2 snaps It's gone in an instant

& you back reminiscing Intro Visioning

Sub-consciousness leading. Doubting god-

ness . Intrinsic love goddess.

bruised heart-bleeding

and still wanting you missing the intriguing.

Wondering what's new Your simplicity got me

feenin

lyrics flowing

Love guiding

lesson learning

you surfaced it

& I think it had to be like this Passion igniting

      desire burning my-core

          Magnet reflections

          Hardest lesson is acceptance

yes to your next request for more

Complementary-vibrations. Ancestral-

      relations. Time-space-what could have

      been. Arranged-marriages. Family

      interpretations

And I can't help but think I somehow missed

      my destiny over a drink

Over fear of love-lost overseas

I wonder if corrections are a possibility

Our connections holistically for me therapy

Physically; Equal opposite-energy

Next time I won't chance it

Looking back wishing I shared what was for

  you meant

   What da most high sent

Next time I'm insisting I'll be true

I won't play hide and seek will you

I'll let you see. Come in. Let me lead

Who could stay true? Who could love you for

you? Reciprocity I saw that in you

Who would be just as proud

      DNA coding

Who don't like crowds

Dignified blood speaking out loud

I'm drawn to you from history. Look at us

now

Let the most high will be done

Let I become one with the one

To learn lessons through experience and gain
a wise dome

Real lessons in life don't play. you can get it
today you can see it yesterday no more game
face. just reality. all day

p.o.a.

Point of Attractions shift so easy.

I dip so low with ease

Falling towards the shadows endlessly

I almost had it. I thought I released baggage

but I let it slip. Innate confidence I lost my

grip

Thinking I slid passed never blaming them or

you

Knowing it was mine own. Responsibility.

Corrections. Self- evaluations. Love bubbling

Africa seeking. What was I thinking?

that everything would fall in. That you needn't
daily seek protection even in Zion?
Thinking dis land is holy Bare-feet
Not realizing it's a battle beyond physicality
Asking for wisdom more than once a week
Necessary
Discretion. Most high you choose for me
Relations
Acquaintance
Physical attractions

you know better I'm weak
Reacting to loneliness
when it's just you I need
Angelic interpretations

Speak through vibrations

Open my eyes

Looking in 3 and 4d

Glasses bi-focally

2 lenses

1 screen

Double consciousness. Filling with creativity

Waiting to return to me

Maybe it's just an end

Mistaken

Thinking dis was where it begins the new

african me. Most High I'm asking for

clarification

I ain't bulletproof. No vest-protection

Shells sticking too. stitches can't mend

Spiritual war

ain't fair

Parallel experience and dreams

Foes

Friends. In an instant Attacking

No time to lose just reflexes. Offense

When my light starts to pierce the air

4th chakra retaliations

Metaphysical weapons aimed towards they

      glare

Threatening

Vampires stare. Suck energy. Blood feenin

Seeking. Faking friends. Listen b

when you hearing

your soul speaks clear

Watch out when they disappear

Then come around again

Nighttime lurking

Searching for open auras. Active chakras

Heart beating. Cold air. Foggy breath

Off track in the forest-shivering. G-p-s
                    working-less

The only way I know is from whence

Looking back Sodom burning
            These are the facts

Empires rise & fall throughout history what
            about that

Where you want to be at?

Cradle of humanity.Un-colonized safety?

Soul snapping fingers impatiently

Thinking 'bout returning

Babylon illusions sodium-luring

I'm thirsty for that sweetness I felt early

Facts more reliable than dreams

Reflecting reminiscing

Experience teach lessons painfully

Floating backtracking

Grass ain't neva green. Point of reference

What's green to you Yellow & blue deceptions

Giving impressions

That this is it

When it's multiplied to infinity

We do create life vibrating beings

Experience from outward in and the opposite
again
Awareness singularity moving independent
Molecules in a peitrie dish
spinning and attaching to its complement
Creating worm-holes for transmuting
Matter into energy then reversing
Translating light into thoughts
External and internal Vibrating rhymes
Ready for reclusions
Wonder who's losing Him or me
Whose really choosing?
When I'm clearing just reacting
That's not the same as creating, you gotta see

That transmutation comes from nothing but

source

God particles from deep

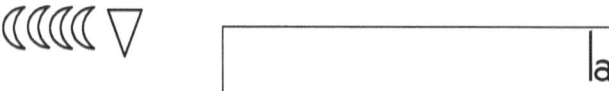

New feelings. Implied reasoning's
Playing along.
Your kindness toppling my walls
Smiles, comforting my insecurities
Looking through me
Detecting my light
Encouraging
Like your friend gone you keep reminding
Similar quotations. Frustrations
Hand gestures. voice manipulation
Terminology got me reminiscing
Missing
Touches familiar sex tingling missions

The way he was so real. Foundation

Sensing your guys appeal

Easy female grabbing. Un- enthused

Quiet solitude

What's up with you two?

Different physiology. No blood relations

Am I viewing your energy towards me deepen

or lessen?

Guessing

got me reminiscing bout how I felt with him

Wondering when I'll get my revelation

you two toppling expectations

I know there's a reason

Time-space calculations. Our presence

Future relations possibilities weaken

What about him?

we ain't nothin

I'm looking for something lasting Like real

friends

your boyish relations

Sucking me in

Ok y'all both want mi what then?

How long will it last really? Conversations

missing what you thinking baby

It can't just be for teasing what we consider

violation

Your phrases taking me back

To what I'm missing Bout him

Passion Black Ecstatic orgasms

Melanated bodies and they shine

Antennas curling Signaling the divine
Fire and h2o combined. Connections
Me and this dude now playing silent attraction
Magnets being led. Mental debating
Eyes speaking words unsaid
2months of space maintaining
Both joy-lacking. Missing. Texting. Waiting
Bodies needing physical attention
Distance stretching
Friends and lovers fading.
Boundary pushing leading towards
acceptance
Loyalties. Outside misconception importance
lessens
My participation

No justifications
Adults consenting
Plus he aforementioned
Possibilities
Us linking after he leave offerd maturely
knowing we'd get along but I'm weary
I think they stage setting
Want an eventual three-some, gaming
betting
So young but capacities go beyond
Mere manipulation. Psychology teaching
unexpectedly
Good loving abilities-geography
unveiling what's possible realistically
Mind restrictions lifting

Bridges building. No stigmatizing
These dudes got me wishing. I can have two
Queenly satisfaction. Perceptions
Indoctrinations. Social implications
What's wrong and right mixing
Pros and cons Evaluations
Higher thinking
Esoteric living

Walking slumber

Subconscious navigating

Yet incomplete puzzles

Divine light

Descending towards humanity

Fixated on confused ideas of spirituality

mortality

individuality. When actually

We are one with all things

Here observing and participating

Opinions bombarding

Socializing. Conformities. Insecurities leading

Deceiving

Hearts hardening

When loneliness sinks in
And family seems distant. And lips start
quivering. I too easily forget from whence
Now feeling trapped in another type prison
Wisdom flows through experience
Hope by a need of something to depend
Grass green temperaments. drinks clouding
        intuition
            Holistic decisions
Trying to remember details to no avail
The first bad conscious dream I don't want to
know or tell. Actions seeping in setting up shit
Remembering bits

9:46

I am done

U run to the front save the bottle at the bar

I get in the car

turn over to sleep short trip

Remember vaguely in the car talking shit

my purse on my arm. cell phone. got my keys

Me stepping in. Cold-granite. Bare-feet

Heading to the guest-bed

Laying down too swiftly. sitting-up chuck-ing

Midnight missed call-relative space and timing

Language boundaries-binding

all of a sudden my words ain't getting through

sketch

where's my shit

he wouldn't bet
he's was my stand-in
this was a set

figured a massage would get me beyond
was it my massage or was I dreaming?
fucking liqs setting me up and now my own
memory I can only half-trust
soul's journey diverts like a dream in disguise
his six-packs got me looking-down
need to be looking in eyes
taking notes
        with disappointing sighs
Respect the god first then get respect outside
how many times must I realize

lessons pressing

contextual elevations

Divine expectations

Life teachings

Angelic beings Unto earth heading for

redeeming

For a moment Until they begin believing

That this is all there was to be and

responsibilities they release

for human sub-serving

Treasonous dealings

Seems like holly-weird scenes. Watching and
        believing yet distractions teaching

Redemption

Esoteric dealings

Return me back to me so I can forget these

bad-dreamings

| im confessing |

I tried denying. It's your energy magnetizing

Subatomic particle attractions

Cellular connections lead to physical interactions

First night, I told myself we'd never again meet

grinning of the henny. your flavor intrigued.

Privileged youth. Rebel mentality.

Sensed your immaturity. Felt it when we was dancing. Your hands tryna undress feeling up my crevices. Expecting to sing so easy. Dangerousness.

You ask if I want to roll, I agree. Thinking how I dodged sum dread wanna-b. But it was jus the beginning.
You hit me after three weeks
I pick up accidentally…Destiny reminding
You were cordial. I spoke politely
Tonight I ain't got nothing better to do
We ate blaze sip on sum booze
Check in to a bomb suite. California king
Milk white feather down inviting me
Huge mirrored vanity flat screen

I approved silently.

Settling back watch my reflection across the bed

You climb forward. I release my straps. Nothing said

You rapped

we sung till *leleet*

Checking out before morning got too deep

I went home. we linked.

In the car hyena watching. Outskirts of the city

Pushing towards the Africa I'd been longing to see

Feet banging the ceiling of your CRV

you had something to prove. I had nothing to lose

Yogi flexibility. You push my legs back but ain't check

with me. Small space long limbs

Fucked up my lower 13. 2 weeks. Low back problems

Is the universe punishing

I try to release, break the link, distract myself, think.

Cellular attraction keeping me synced

You keep calling. shit fuck me

My feelings rise

Hypnotized. Is it lust or life. Day dreams with

bedroom eyes. We were friends in disguise

Likened to the wind

Till a breeze blows in

And you start coasting, forgetting origins

You sank out at sea

come back me bout a breeze that hit last week

Fucked up trees. put you in emergency. Sudden death,

but by chance no damage detriments. Jasmine still

fresh

Next scene

Nurse warns the Queen. B look left. I say don't fret.
You say it was your ex. You did make contact. She
was here. Now she left
Game. Stamped. Set. Salute. Ras-spect

Signs recurring. Ignorance flowing
Audacity illuminating. Temptation luring
And we sung. Both understanding the relations
You fuck up again
Your contact in my fone changes
Now your pings read: *Udunwitdat* ringing

Experience teaches wisdom it's time for you to learn
the womb is not a swap. You are a gardener

You just a son. You ain't know my flex

Greet, touch, protect. Anything I want I get

Conscious contentions anytime we link

You me plus the henny equal b turn freak

Reality reminding logically

Accepting responsibility even just partly

I gave you a break that lasted a week

You asked me over to your place for a drink

Insisting when I'm tryna resist, Charming

Invite my puppy along, genuinely heart-warming

Can't help but concede. Seems you beginning to see

Thin ice small thread line you walking-mistaking a

queen

Herb, Saharan breeze, Garden setting star gazing
You got me giggling. We retreat. Sing till leleet
I got a chance to sleep. I feel nothing I think
You cook for me.
My tummy and the sea. Zebee. French kitchen. Chef
qualities.
My hunger and heart swelling. Undress you with my
eyes. Your confident stride
Soon forgetting hunger highs.

Ready for the next session, making silent confessions
Wanting you pressed against me, loving the
indiscretions. You seeming more than 23,
imagining last week's lesson
my face against the wall

Your stiffness booty tracing

Our geometric lap. Pyramidal stack. Ass up head

down-fingas up, brace my back

180 degree high

Currents racing

Bodies shaking/Belly button tickling/Eyes closed

giggling/Hearts beating/ sweat beading/waters

rushing/no restrictions.

My lips become the lift

elevating us beyond what's current

Identities. Undressed soul revealing; though you keep

hiding. masculine explanations. ego justifications…

When love is set free from defense and opens up

anew; Paradigms and elevations shift

Galactic reasoning-Inward conversations   shit.

New friends

Smiles lead to darkened dens

Eyes twinkling

Bodies' feenin

Drinks convoluting previous aura-cleaning

De-toxing emotional-dealings. Negativity

Fighting off lonely feelings

Lifted from meditations

Ready for love interactions

Floating. Lights beaming

Envisioning Africa as Eden

Expecting the same and linking

Intrigue stifles me till they start with they

delusions

Cave-neander beings-2 greedy

Scarcity thinking. My soul weeping

Knowing divinity. Queenly-living. Sanctity

The wails are deafening

They say remember me

Remember you were never lonely

Remember your king

Remember righteous living

When it was just about 3 things

     sleep

     cheese

          and time quality

Now being sapped electrically. Standards &

beliefs. Finding less than I've saw or seen

Learning lessons

Leaving regret beyond social conceptions

Focused on light permeating manifestations

No more walking blind

The source touched my eyes

Now I got night-vision

 ## catchin feelings

Comfy yet awkward relations and dealings

Holding back

 don't want to expose my heart beating

Knowing love can grow from sex infatuations

Body-feenin

Heart wanting more fronting like I'm not

thinking

bout us rising Beyond realms

Physicality. Contracts. Semen's. Zygote

conceiving

It's not a trap. It's more like we just match

I want to delete all my contacts

Tell 'em fuck off it's a wrap. If you really

got my back

Right now my comfort is shaky. Cus when

I'm with you I don't wanna leave baby

Plus with your mind I'm intrigued

Catching feelings

you being younger don't even matter to me

Daily musings

Once every 2 weeks ain't enough I got greed

Yet initially we chose to concede

Steaming ahead chemistry-led

No emotions

Can I release my heart- leak- potions

Mind insisting

   B don't catch feelings

Why you made my year when you came back

to da city

After I released you from my seams
Realized all connections are temporary
Now you back confusing me mentally
New conclusions

      Yes we are meant to be linking
Then 2 lose you locally on some dumb-shit
drinking. I ain't tell you a quarter of what I
been thinking. I ain't give you a proper
welcome. Learning lessons

            Bout heart distractions
Reality stems from dreams
To receive you must release
Tell me you weren't thinking
That magnetism been our thing
That it wasn't cosmic chemistry

when we released

That synchronicity been guiding

That us relating ain't just about carnality

That love shows up un-expectedly

That bonds can lift stress and anxiety

That we can teach each other real shit quietly

That you a prince and I'm royalty

That if you open up your heart you got my
loyalty

That we here to love create and be
Free from boundaries

you excite me more than you think

Catching more feelings with your integrity

perspective shifting

Consciousness building

Egos diminishing

Floating

While ships sinking

Out here its work and play

Disturbing scenes another day

My light shining melanin detecting

Oneness seeking

Why I keep linking with lower end beings?

Caught up in the experience and believing

That this is it

That a woman is a bitch

That pussy come second

Phallic complexes

One night I thought I saw a sign

A dark reflection

What used to be mine heights

What are the odds me meeting my type

With-out taking a flight

Foreign circumstances

Common DNA lines

Blackness

Eyes slanting

Doberman like

Clean

Pressed

Fresh kicks

Faded sides

Red and black

Miami ties

Everything falling in line

And I been open

Body yearning

Needing attention cuddling caressing

Memories stirring

Remembering love again

My Adam

Original masculine

His missile swelling

And I can't believe I left him

Meeting disappointment after dissing the one

      appointed

Divinely

Historically

My king

Throne building

Balanced

Hu

Sa

Queen complementing

Here waiting

My patience

Leaking and peaking

Male friends faking

Egoist banking planning-drinking

        smiling

                smoking

                        waiting

For chemical reactions

Mad I don't give it to dem

Pissed that it's my choice

That liquor won't do me in

The power struggle in silence

They mental frustra-tions

Too thirsty for respect expecting

Blinded to the scene

        Angels terra walking

                Sprite serving

Light sharing

Really caring. Ready to reason

Exchanging diasporic commonalities

        Repatriation

           Garvey

              Malcom

But there's too much resistance

Calcifications

Fluoride and sweets deactivating

Un-learning

mind-wealth depreciations for temporary

moments

I'm like a flute player and he's a snake

Forgets to strike or strikes early

                              not late

Basic standards they neva meet. I stopped

measuring

My theory It's an epidemic culturally

          Historic empire stretching

Europe and Asia mixing

Manhood's shrinking

Tendencies Roman

Coliseum

Olympics

Fascination with sticks

Female theatrics

Neurons disconnected

A pint of blood for each completion

Towards viagra heading

Are these the pre-perverted-old-men

Consciousnesses built on making up for

      what's lacking

Loving up they friends

don't know how to plant a seed

not real

just pretend

Tension they love to seek

Indoctrinations

they import from overseas

Where am I?

Is the most high revealing?

Grass gets green with watering

It's the same sun beaming and burning

Nutrient feeding

Sa transforming

Gases floating

Towards the beginning

Source

Magnetizing

Particles reconnecting and

      remembering divinity

Liquefying

Gravity pulling

Ready to experience love again

Creation from a different perspective

Soul tapping

New and ancient situations emerging

Lessons to carry into eternity

Open to manifest. To learn again

Separating only temporarily

Knowing. Lights on no dimming

Promising to never to forget beginnings

H2o got memory

Liquefying. Womb cleansing.

Divine concept-ting

Soul solidifying. Un-veiling wisdom

Ancient over-standings

Love and oneness the only medium

so sweet

Most high are you playing with me

After so much rain you send the sun

Like Abyssinian summers after winter season

Rays lacing Like DNA strands

Permeating bands linking

I feel my aura expand

Like Sirius A & B

Binary stars dance around me

Like flowers stretch toward source

Magnetized

Love's guide is getting me high

Naturally

Like orbs disguise passed lives & vibes

Spiritual presence in photos can't see with the

        naked eye

Like that

        We're floating towards the sky

Appearing in an instant

He got me to listen

Patient

The strong & silent type

Afraid to look in his eyes

        It's like he seeing through

Glass is beautiful but it break too

Every word he speak have meaning

             Tongue tamed

Integrity drawing me in

                    I almost forgot the rain

Feelings rising by the second. Tryin to hide

Free enough to say the truth gen

Like he's under my skin

                    Human lie detection

My face the screen

& he's monitoring in silence

Needles jump pulse rates increase

Body tensing then relaxing with release

Bound to former understandings

Societies

Keeping me below the higher me

        Love is all we need

Been thinking bout how you move inside

Yes

   Even when there's no light

Our bodies shine

Bet

Finger grazing sparks

    Static cling

      Like fire flies

We make our own electric streams

Opening hearts Laser beams

   Raising hips

Adjustments

   Fitting perfect

Yang & yin

Metaphysical surgeons

Healing hearts, bodies & emotion

Sweat beading

Goose bumping

Shivers running

Blink twice

Look up towards the ceiling

Focus dilation

Face to face

Brown eyes

His confidence oozing

Intent on performing

The gaping hole

In my heart Now closing

Gratefulness overflowing

Your patience. Been lonely

Holding out for my complement

8-2-sixing only

Chakras reflecting Mirroring intuitions

New forms of communication

Let me know what you thinking

Ladies and emotion

Solar plexeze ears open

What's the cost of wisdom Solomon

Sheba is coming

Leading armies

Soldiers following

Higher thinking

Exemplifications

All eyes and attention

Discernment wisdom

Righteousness

Intention

Empress by blood Not by relation

Ancient knowledge

Mind sexing Attracting bodies

Biology. Truth is freedom. No more bondage

 lyrics

I stay with dem too

Lyrics ain't few

It's our story

Ancient memory

DNA whispers. Flashbacks & day dreams

Times passed. Experiences beyond these

lights

Scenes flash behind our eyes like a

movie screen. Families' dignitaries

Strategically

Kingdoms align

Empire ties

Dis da one for you

Dis family

Dat genetic string

Dis bloodline

Dem know which recipe

Baking queens & kings. Compatibility

Tribes alliance

Height

Complexions. Abyssinian curing in silence

Purifying

Dignitaries

Worldly

Back to Africa

Poetry writing

Shakespearean Amharic speech

Ras

Dejazmach

High ranks

Fighting with pride alone. No tanks

Boundaries stretch

Crown prince and princess

That would have been us

Thrones built and set

God fearing. Classes complement

When the ancestors speak thru us

Telling stories. We at they feet

Soaking ancient energy

Bout how it used to be

     Arranged marriages

Based on more than carnality

Families linking children

                   Maintaining royalty

Blood rushing thru us

                   H2o got memory

For at least the next generation to know

& not believe. Medieval origins. Financial

relations property. Ties to the king

Sheba and Solomon

That's who we are Yet I think we fell far

Lost it. Forgot it. Bought into they lies

Babylon misguides. Dancing with opposing

sides. Conditioning. Adapting. Illogically

We justify. Ignoring whispers

Ignorance ripping souls in two

Drowning out ancestral pride & cries

Good thing DNA can't deny

& h2o got memory

So we can't keep up the lies

For long

Slave songs

Mourning loudly, clouding the journey that

could have led to edges. Fog. Castles

The Atlantic. Sending us out to the sea

Before ultimate sufferage

Lashes

400 more years till waking

Conscious less

Soul breaking

Spirit beings

Terra walking

Kingz & queens historic memory

Vibrating thru you & me till infinity

Whispering silently

Eternally guiding

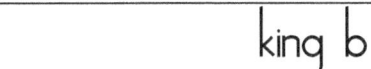
king b

Betty da truth more like a fable

Tryna box me up labels.

Led from creation. Cosmic dust. Stable vibrations

Fuck what they thinking. If you listen you

hear him

Reminders in the present you thought you knew me.

Past life-parallel dimensions. DNA stir memories

Flash

look into my eyes

Crystal balls drift us back

Familiar scenes got me in a trance
Dejavu. Me on my back
Your stance. The way you tell me to relax
Your tone. Desert sands African lands
Inhaling your scent
I taste the herb on your breath
Sweat seeps thru skin. Pelvis lifts independent
Tongue traces. No acrylics. No brushes
Your muscle in between spreading seas
heat eruptions

emissions splatter canvas like Polluck.
Artistic genius; like clouds floating by
then they gone in an instant
Abstract installations. Fine art is priceless

One night

Private viewing

One gallery

Two invitations

Waters rush north like the Nile. Hold it in

Chakras rise & balance aligning meridians

Pumping estrogen. Testosterone feeding feminine

Liquid into gases building bridges; Hemi-syncing

Telepathic conversations. Pollinations

Mating season

Medieval living

Royal families linking

Zion at the core

One aim

Protect your queen-dome

Could have been the case if we listened
If revolutions ain't change shit
If former generations
weren't duped into western promises
to see what
emigrating does to families
Morphing DNA with hormones
Redefining mo-rality
Social conditioning. Thrones built no seats
When you can trace royalty DIRECT in your
genes
Royal suns bowing down to neander-beings
Accepting crumbs before setting out to sea

Repa-triation

Garvey Malcolm & Me

Abyssinian sovereigns back spitting poetry

Lyric rhymes. Describing times

Former institutional lines

Soldiers marching East. Orien's belt. 1 2 3

Sirius A & B

Queens running so much shit

they called them king

So from onward in dats me

Betty da truth aka King B

Cosmic origins. Orbiting. Transiting

dimensions

Space station monitoring

Vibes

Ties

Relations

Lighting infatuations

Consciousness descent. Ions. Love elevations

Astro-professions. Moon cultivating

Mars destinations

Unified with creation

Descending for an instant

Shooting stars cosmic storming

translating Ge'ez to trees man

It's funny when the student supersedes

those who teach them

Lesson plans

Higher conscious demands

Reflecting source

Out living

Sacred geometry

3 plus 3 eons and still growing

Roots grounded source energy surrounded

Giving off vibes You exist for a reason

Give thanks

Hugging trees

former students exemplify

the teacher's original lead

Now searching for what they taught

Before they got lost

Flash

2016

Ranges

Land plots

Industry

Scramble for Addis

Foreigners vs. me

Fantasy vs. reality

Proof seeking youth running free

Cash

Girls posted on the street

Coke

Weeknd

MTV

80 million ears & attention

Pill popping

Female value dropping

Clock ticking

Lavas rushing to streams trickling to the

Serengeti

I keep dem confused Un-intentionally

My-complement male-energy

My muses add to my bluesy medz

Experience teaches wisdom

So at least my loss was less

even fucked-up shit inspire my pen

Moving slowly. they running like a track meet

Slow down homie. talk is cheap

Satisfaction temporary. not tryna take me

out to eat

Or even

check me during the week

Theatrics

Pouting

Insulting intelligences

Points dropping by the second

Talking bout I'm playing him

Yet we attract our reflection

You want me to stay in the dark

Here's a j boo let's spark

Rub on my booty this way

Stretch my limbs for da gym later today

sweet words all you need to say

That's my four thru 12- play

Let me sleep

don't ask to fuck

Tryna keep my number down. Not up

That's just your bad luck

Neva bet on me you lose

thinking this smile is confused

Neva that blazed or boozed

And I don't care if you frustrated sexually

I had to get used to dat too

What I do stick & move

Re-focus pass thru

If it was really meant to be

No convincing necessities

We woulda been between the sheets

resort beach-breakfasting

Insisting I get comfy now sit

shine a black light on dis bed I'd bet it light up

Vegas strip

But he got it twisted tryna put it on me

Talking shit

Not asking just assuming before he flip

Crying I'm the bluffing one

Like I ain't got nothing betta to do

Than to lead you on & run

Gaming

like us chilling was for just my fun

Enjoying company no-sex play

Making solo-contracts binding without letting

me read

It's your mind playing you homie

Not me

Maybe I play betta than you on da life board

We playing with chips when your ass need a
sword

Dis a two person game like chess

Gage your options

Move forward

Review

you underestimate competition

And like poker nigga you lose

Mistaking the queen's authority

Resisting when the body speaks up

Booty pushes back at the the gentlest touch

Lips pursed shut while reflexes give me up

Looking in my eyes when we talk

Game up

The weeks

the cold bed

patience b

defense penetrations

Remembering what happened;

similar scenes Quotations

Body weak Heart wounded

Mind justifying fogging logic

Integrity testing

Tactile sensations tempting

Unspoken curiosity

Until they on to the next n I'm deplete

Alone shivering

Disturbing scenes

Lessons regurgitating

Abyssinian queen don't need shit

Mixing with civilians

Fuck that

Suck a dick

Next time

I appreciate

What I got before it's gone

Next time I'll just be happy to give my king

a sun

Love too precious to find when you dig

Move slow

Don't crack it

Crystals release energy

Heart beats likewise attract it

grateful

Thinking of you my heart begins to swell
Thinking of you can send me deep into a well
Every emotion
I could sell
Dripping with truth
Genuine natural deposits
Resources hidden from view
Our first moment
How from them time I knew

You were the one I had been searching
longing to meet my other half my other me
Your strength, your sincerity
Spoke to me silently
Your eyes said I knew you in a dream
Love kept eluding me

I became content at waiting
Or being alone simply

When I think of you my senses peak
When you leave even for a moment; I feel like
surgery
When you return my glee is before me
You are my treasure like a pot of gold I found
you. You found me

Your lips take me to ecstasy
Our hearts beat simultaneously
Organs mix our chemistry
In a lab creation of what could be
If we let the most high lead
If we let the most high lead

100 choices

If I have to choose a hundred times
I'd choose you to the end
You are the epitome of how a king can be a
civilian
How your lips smirk
How you make my hips jerk
Just one touch sends tingling sensations
I'm tryna express what's in the silence
But words have not been created. We have
our own language

Those who don't know can't guess
That love is not a war
It's a conquest
To conquer it Is not to leave

To win is to stay though it shakes you
egotistically
Former thinking questioning
Who you thought you were. Who you'd
otherwise be
Without love we're in disguise
How do you know what you would do
Until you turn the mirror to reflect the
truth…that is you standing in the way
Image…Social conditions..Indoctrinations
All refuting Love's existence

Angels manifest to show you the way
                  but we are tossed aside
They do the worst
                  to those who are kind
They ravage like serpents
                        Blind
Contrast
Contradictions
Made visible by loves existence
God never blamed the lost

Both he and they know what would be the
cost
If they stray from love
                              If they never trust
But love gave me better when I gambled
Though through the muck I scrambled
Hoping to gain love from lust
Never came up
Just some more bad luck
proof fiends
But angels don't compete they intrigue and
leave…No struggle…No animosity
Love's Purpose more important
Focus energy-preservation
Change your thinking
          Change your reflection

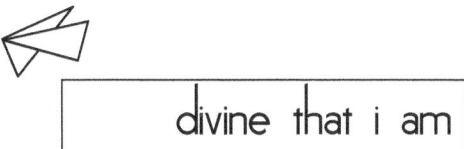

divine that i am

I compliment all man

Divine that I am

The empress upon which all stand

Divine that I am

The style's designing hand

Divine that I am

The beauty of all lands

Divine that I am

The highest holy lamb

Divine that I am

The ancient origins

Divine that I am

The deepest lover's friend

Divine that I am

The never ending wind

Divine that I am

That graces all your skin

Divine that I am

Submits to her King essence

Divine that I am

And leads with silent reverence

Divine that I am

That drinks from her-own floods

Divine that I am

And showers all with love

Divine that I am

She brings forth temptations

Divine that I am

Creates magnetism

Divine that I am

Who is fed and who she feeds

Divine that I am

Knows when to follow and when to lead

Divine that I am

She truly is the queen

Divine that I am

From which come forth everything

Divine that I am

visualization

What u want to see and
following thru
With activation

I felt u but my eyes didn't see
thought it was just fantasies
taunting me

my mind couldn't accept
that I could win*Lose
then come back To win

but when u hold on to love
possibilities are limitless

Naysayers make bets
others scoff
bad mind intents

Tryna throw you off

I knew u were mine
because years ago I asked
If lies were the facts
and if love could truly ever
lead mi off path

And if dreams and reality can
converge and orgasms can
take me upwards

focus
is a thing
u gotta hold strong
it will try and fade u
Lest it string u along
its mission can kill u
Some never return
some can't take the sting
Of that first hot love burn
but when u pass through the
pain and u stay on your track

Love will always guide u right
back. that's what I know
experience. when u gain it
u grow

Chakras can get u in a bind
waste your time
get u to believe lies
get u to cross enemy lines
unjustly justify
simple minds
lower self on the rise
spirits demise

But there is a silver line
when u know where u been
observing winds
change of times...fluidity
what's real to you
to me illusionary
this experience who they think
they see
time and space

Separating aspects of mi
u never knew I was just
passing

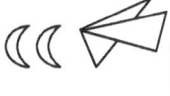

remembering

Forehead kisses

Body twists

Your hands

Your lips

Your touch

My hips tingling

I wanna release you

       Forward marching

         Debating

Risk a text or call for more disappointment

           & waiting

Making mistakes is so new to me

Learning curves don't exist in life I see

Losing 1 thing that was real

      Even semi

Did you release the reflections

Do you remember my lips & our love

                           connections

Couldn't I in a brief moment also slip

But our shit was cosmic

Or was it just me

Swirling

Sweating

Burning

Internally meditating on the stars

          Body stretching

                        Wetting
Tryna release

                                        Tryna raise kundalini
                        Get lifted
Tryna rise esoterically
                        Pelvis shift-ments
Romantic riddims
Vibrations
Getting me high
Straight addicted
                                        Feenin
Sex mystics
                Physics
                        Sound
movement

Power in the darkness

Our

      bodies become harps

                man

Singing praises

Creation

Melanated

Masculine and feminine

One Maestro blending

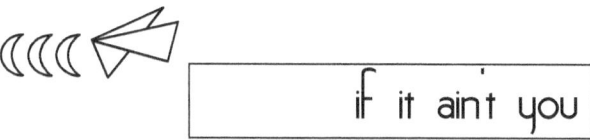

if it ain't you

I'm just passing thru

Never stopping to dream

They ain't even come close for comparisons

Never even chasing...these cats will never

know they missed the race and

they only good for one reason

no point in speaking so why they lips keep

     moving?

My eyes looking thru...Obliviousness

you walking aim less too...Mistaking love for

     sex

Hoping to draw me in a web

        Spiders spinning lies they used

to fool they-own heads

Flesh. No consciousness

Hearts via eyes

My soul connect my thighs

Different imaginations

Dimensions

        Space and time

Mental distance while niggaz talking I don't

    listen

    cause my hearts in a deep depression

Sunken post-volcanic eruptions

Water filling what used to pump-blood

esoteric-calculations

Destiny rejuvenation

Life's truest ambition

To discover the heights of intention others

        walking victim

Devaluing elevation for ego substantiation

Mistaking gods for civilians

Under-estimations

Till I snap back

I'm leaving

Like a breeze like the suns retreat-westing

Heavens setting I'm remembering-Love

most high guide

Teach me

Reveal

Whats lacking

Unveil my happy ending

I have these feelings

But manifestations

They keep eluding

Distractions convoluting

Can't do a thing with-out cheeze

Boredom weakening

Attracting low vibrating beings

1st chakra maintaining

Smiling winking feeding drinking

Before disappearing easy

No more please..No texting

Ain't know a goddess when they meet

Here for brotherly living

eyes looking blindly

ears need volumes increased

I'm sinking

Lessons for learning

Ready for Atlantic-swimming

Grabbing up my lost king

Here astray from me I keep losing

Observing trying not to engage deep

short attention

I want the life I'm supposed to be living

Extending my reach

Now noticing which events

Feelings babylon mis-dealings

Under-standings....thought combos

Formerly could lead Contradictions

Africa seeking Babylon confusing

Economic inhibitions. Kingly in-securing

Taxing my spirit. Waiting for reunifications

Spiritual manifestations. Divine living. No

drinking. Monk-like living. Children. Peace of

mind

Independently financed

Fluidity

Open signs

Intuition

Be my guide

Completely

Cosmic memory

Re-align my-mind

my conscious

Staring me in the face

Opposing my earthly ways

Insisting I just be

Soul snapping fingers impatiently

Eyes looking deep

Attracting

Flesh feeling weak

Surface drifting

Periodically diving

Before floating

Unrevealing while undressing

Invisible sheets

Fear fighting

Therapy sessions

Conscious deconstructing

Masks

Walls

Insecurities hiding

With one smirk

I change the subject

Flesh defending

Soul penetration

Lips kissing to keep from thinking

Bout decisions

Sway-ing the ocean

Heart wishing

Body feenin

Love dreaming

Connections reaching

You give what you get

Bandaging wounds with ribbons

Wondering why healing never began

Who is it I am

Where are my real friends

When does attraction turn to love

Will my past stay unresolved

Why my options stay stalled

When will I manifest god

When will frustration cease

When to reveal innate abilities

And he said

When I won't settle

When I do better

When I stop hiding

When I quit lying

love's hostage

It's a war outside

It's miry

Its divide

It's a union mixed with pride

Who will win?

Who knows

Lovely understated

It's a thing to be debated

When two come together in a
cloud And soar

Before dropping ground-ward
Honey I don't want to be a
hostage to your love

Held up by fantasies Merely holding on to see

It's me who I need Not dreams

Feelings clouding Distracting reality

Masking what's before With sentimentality

What I thought was love Was only ego lifting

A soul far from home Sea separating

Father/daughter debating

                             Hearts at its peaks

When love was just a family completely

Daddy tending his garden Raising two flowers
skywards Stretching for his warmth Stems releasing
past living Past hurt unforgiving

                             See me I want this cycle to end

                             Sex or love A barter's pretend

Is a joke existence When
there's heaven in Eden

And hearts swelling at your
presence When roses grow in
bunches of three Rejoicing at
creation

Rays and rain giving nutrition

Oh what a blessing it was
When we remembered true
love was not a man made
glee….It was a part of nature
Indiscriminately

And we felt it for a moment

Then we were swept under
some tree

and now came to believe that

this life...this reproducing

this sharing mixed with bartering Was worth the pain because we now we hold the reigns

To sweep over new trees Or disguise the losses with materialism Or strive for simple idolatry

Money and people worshiping

Drinking and eating what *they* say

Who *they* put before me

Not the one who truly gives times 3

Who's watched your conception and protected

Who comforted your tears Who's been there all those years What a disgrace When money takes that place

Conscious morbid living

Patience depleting Condemning silently

Until a soul retires Tired of the falsity

In a moment we are driven back

A seed

Birthed to flourish

No longer learning

Just knowing

That it is a gift to be anything in a world created
perfectly

To sparkle From absorbing

Releasing god energy

Creation Mother naturally in me

Unending Over willing to close the cycle

What was lost was a gain

All her hurt A lessen

For seeds to stretch again

Towards the one who first knew them

Love

jah

Haj

Ha

Ahh

Mmm

Vibrating

Historic humming

Heaven's journey

Masses from particles

Meditations

Remembering when the power
was in our hands

Above mounds

Looking down

Feeling sound

Breathing winds in and out

Cosmic storms

Crashing chaos into norms

Focused attention

Creators magnifying

Peering directing senses

Visually defining creatures

Light artists

Perfecting their creations in
our essence

Meant Not to lament

To find what's sent

For them only Patient

Life can lead to millions

Life can give you cents

But what happened within

Did you listen

Did you trust that the air
wouldn't end

It didn't

Your lungs your active
transmission

Air your lubricant

Your water to quench

Red blood cells active

Functioning digestive system

Nucleus and atoms

Sexual organs too

wigodyou

Electrons and protons

On the grind non-stop

How much would you pay

if you were their boss

Organizing the chaos

For your gain

do you love them

or for-granted do you take
them

Hurdling through space

Anything can happen

Nuclear waste leaking

Earth shift off rotation one
inch

and shit change

And maybe your environment
can't hang

And it's another ice age

Or volcanoes erupt

Underground earth quakes

Plates dip

What was a mountain now a
rift

Lions take their grips

Nuclear bombs slip

And we back to

Energy gases

Focused on sources

Creation

No hands

No digs

Bursting and releasing like
your own body-function

Electricity creating

Blood pumping

Cells divide

Proteins bind

Nutrient feeding

Flash a split second

Into an atom

Passion

Exchange

Working functionally

Chaos organizing quickly

Time is a gift

Don't waste it

In a flash you're dead

Space capsule operations

Highs speed

got a team working tirelessly

To keep you alive

Space suits zipped tight

you wanna see the universe

Look inside

Finish the game your only
mission's guide

Breathing the storming Chaos

Bliss

Peace

Haj

Jah

Ha

Ahhh

Om

Mmmm…

uncertain

Certain people got game
Certain folks just pretend
Certain conversation spreads
Certain understandings
Full steam ahead
Certain uncertainties

Afraid to question
They ain't know they core of belief
Scared of what may start leakin
So they stay on they pc
Correct politics
Kids stay tricked with TV
Families support regression

They ain't know no other lesson
Certain vibes
Certain lifestyles
Surface floating
Fear trauma jealousy greed
Homes breaking at the seams
False-ness gloating
No love energetically

No reaching out and assisting
Tryna remold the most-high creation
But they can't see or praise them
Blind to they own deficiencies
Standard adopting
Ignorant masses following
Ain't know who they want to be
Tryna change me
Spoon fed n full of hypocrisy
Msnbc meditating
Cnn regurgitating
Debating
Corporate interest
Every new story advertisement

Memorization
Thinking da lead's in the back
Sleeping dead energy
Robotic acts
Babylonians interfacing
Claiming god's they dad
Exhibiting Satan's deeds
Ego feeding
Smiling lips
Twisted hearts
Dark
How long will it last
What's up with mortality
If u never rise passed

3 rd dimensionality
Never question reality
Glorifying ignorancies
Roman tendencies
Sheep being led
Corn fed on corporate intricacies
Conspiracy blind
Spiritually declined

Uncertain souls
Deemed to return
A second and third thousand
time

shakey investments

Niggaz be investing in pussy
den get mad it don't return

Every investment is a bet no
guarantees niggaz gotta learn

Puff up with they pot bellied
dream

Thinking cash plus food
equates what's in between

They wanna talk investment
but ain't know inflation
schemes

Can't play stocks Sidelined
benched from the team

So they create they own
markets. Tryna create they
own lane

Can't match up competition.
They get pissed and then
complain

Bitchin up when investment
don't return. Before you play
the game, nigga I tell you, you
must learn

Check it stocks rise and fall
with the climate, you ain't
know it

if you wanted something solid,
its only gold or escrow kid

At least then we could both
decide if what you offering is
worth my time. Contracts
bind, negotiations pending ; if
I like then I'll sign. No arms
gotta be bending

But you seem sketch-pyramid
schemes-selling hoop dreams

Perverts waiting to fuck-just to
scream- ego feeding

Currency exchange defined;
you aint know it.

Bartering equals goods
exchanged between patrons.
Balanced contracts show it.

Can't fool me with fine print-
red pen adjustments

Whats that over here? Hell
nah- black out that shit!

Sit back and wait on da review,
patience is a virtue in deals like
dis and poker games too

Too bad the language we
speak ain't da same

I woulda asked why you 50
something playing pussy board
games

So much cash no self esteem.
No queen. Easy bet; 3rd world
chicks be thirsty. For sum
food they give it up.

Based on my seat that's da
card you playing in tha street

But My KING woulda neva
buy pussy like food; he get it
easy

These lazy niggaz ain't living
in reality

They belly exhibits they lack
of rules

No discipline. Addicted to
movies dat is blu

Living all they life with glasses
in that hue. Assuming the
market determines the price of
U cuz that's what they on to.

But international biz lead to
loads

Sumadese hoez hungry; 6
oclock they on da roads

Flagging down diplomats and
tourists in hoe
costumes/competing for
turf/Discipline less. Plain to
see/ Blubber busting they
china seams

Why struggle they say, when
life is a bet

Commodities flooding, half
price- a day's bread

Normalized 6pm views

Bitch Nigga I understand, its
society that's your foe

Fucking with your brain got
you thinking every girls a hoe

Turning you sick. Figuring you
ain't gotta work for it

Got you doing all your
thinking through ur lil dick

It ain't a commodity for me its
lifetime deals. Love is real, but
they will neva know

Focused on they limpness and
how to make it grow

Bellies so big blocking views
And you wanna put all dat
weight on mi Ewww nigga
You confused.

You mixed up a coke bottle shape and a smile

But check it bitch niggaz I sniffed your bitchness from a mile

So investing in me is a tricky game. You want long term dividends, you wanna see how I spend? You want mi to pretend there aint somewhere else Id rather be?

Lunch or dinner 100 USD all you good for. This exchange equates my 1 hour rate. Don't get it twisted nigga. No more.

Accounts real estate economic
freedom When I aim I aint
miss

but with your con-tracts You
need a hoe nigga not a bad
bitch

And you'll get what you
deserve with a turn around the
bend

You give me just enough cash
to come back for a lend

Slavish medz tryna reel mi in.
But that's your problem you
underestimating real-ness

Niggaz don't cry when you
don't return on what you
invest

First check the cents (sense)
Will what you offering gain
interest?

Food and drink I flush down
the toilet. You got money but
aint know your economics.

Fuck your lunch and coffee
appointments. I'm talking
investments foreign. Your
strategy is weak in dis game of
chess. My experience beat you
b-foe you had a chance. You
was chance less.

Good thing too. Cause the rest
that try and match mi I'll
dissect like I did you.

Bisecting contracts

Assumptions don't mean shit
on wall-street

Bell rings before you blink

Look up lost everything

Your former broker escorts
you to the door

You riding subways now no
jets. Anything I want I can get
Nigga bet

Pussy get wet for real niggaz
only

Not bitch niggaz homie

Dropped da mike

Den she left.

mpersonate

Some girls today I don't understand them

A friend to you like Farrakhan was to
Malcolm

Looking to leech and still compete. Rhetoric
and vocal tones of a drag queen

Behavior regurgitations

Long gone it seems are the days when women
strive for unification

Real men watch out cause I see how they play

Bitches be bitches in a real way

Looking to come up offa you

Searching for reasons to keep you spending
Thinking friendship is emotional bending

Love confused with class. A life full of the
cash dash

Bro all I'm saying is watch ur pockets nuff
Cause a new bitch is looking to set you up

Ladies if ya'll ain't making doe. There is no
reason to friend up a hoe

Smiling teeth, wicked schemes, gluttonous
dreams, parched humility. Blind to angelic
meetings.

Forward mover's distant travelers. Common
destinations fuck illusion

living a life of ego proving

When I'm floating by I can only look down
and sigh, cus you think me getting high lacks
depth. Spirit consciousness. No faking. U still
playing I don't smoke herb debating.

It's all in your head, you walking blind,
backwards in time

Neanderthalic ways, looking and sounding
more like a tranny every day

Make up cues and female imitations got you
thinking a Woman is the OPPOSITE dressed
back up again.

*Shaking my head.

Ur socializing impersonations make me weary

Your vibrations are witch eerie

In my day it was about the truth

Assata uplifted the youth

Sistah Souljah opened eyes

Women stood for more than a front

Women used their brains and hearts to exhibit
higher wisdom

But these chicks are lost I'm telling you

Self absorbed and mad you ain't follow

Bitch go your way you won't see me
tomorrow

Life is too short to waste on sleepwalkers

Eyes open focused on increasing vibrations

Cause in a flash it's done and you in a next
dimension

Or you dumb and got left back for a next
session

Maybe then you'll learn.

synchronized

When u talk synchronicity
that's me
I move From dreams to reality
Floating
Abyssinian orbs surrounding
Lights beaming
Vortextually
From deep
Eyes open
All three
Heart ready to receive

Meditations
MY Soul dancing
ecstasy
Electro-magnetic spectrum
Guiding
Equatorial regions bursting

with complementary energy
Making over-standings a
breeze
Rays shining down
I see rainbows
And I'm following THE
sound
MY touch is a blessing
B'cuz i play in gold mounds

Fingers tickle when I'm feeling
free
Tummy tingles alerting danger
n love dealings
Body heats when I wanna get
freaky
Goose pimples rise
Independently
Cheeks flush with shyness
And release
Gentle kisses soften me
Sweet words
intellect

Collecting what's precious
Higher thinking
Eyes peering deep
To uncover truth Behind
smiling teeth
Promising never to be fooled
again
Never 2 just trust Every 1
never believe they only wanna
be friends
Until opportunity rises
And i have less game defense
Training the mind And body
to speak dually
I notice love calling From a
distance
Yet now moving slowly
Resistance easy
When focusing with-in and
Not on just being lonely
But on be-coming simply
Only goodness and peace
energies I Want around me

Maintaining sanctity
I feel my self growing
And Life gives freely what
man only hopes to achieve
physically
When u believe
Wholly

 no one night

I'm tryna come in and step up da ting

Not tryna waste yo time on some one night fling

First thing

When you peering through your lenses

Over stand interpretations is subjective

You see it's your percep-shuns

That keeps you in your pain son

looking out for blind acceptance

That prohibits elevations

You never think how your pain dips into next
generations

You teach them your misdeeds of shame and fear in
blatant silence

You hide instead of exposing your mis-steps

You don't lead like sheep follow

                                you are led

You have to tap into your higher self everyday

You have to sit in silence

                not speak

meditate

You have to listen when your body speaks

You must own your sexual God energy

Know that when you step you simultaneously create

You on nobody's time but your own

It is fake

Don't count on man to acknowledge you are great

When you are already pleasing to the One who first creates

Sweet smelling aromas

Like sage

Cinnamon and rose you emanate

Walk in that knowing

Stay high Procreate

Sex is a healing force like bud on the grave of Solomon

Like bees create honey from sucking out pollon

Like butterfly's cocooning stages

Humans fly into space when orgasms take them

Climaxing on life's breath root sensations

Tactile carrot chasing That is they motivation

When my flesh get mi caught in a funk

I close my eyes and reach down

my spirit button is my cunt

Engineered perfect Nerve endings working

Second chakras pulsing up the rising serpent

Tapped into the all knowing

Will my flesh steal the scene

Or will the mind step in with ideologies

Spirit-self observes contrast

                Judgment a non reality

Constellations whizzing by

Catching one is futile Just try

Accept the beauty you visualize

Take it for what it is

One night teaches more than most university colleges

The chaos in you revealing my own duality

Resistance in mental definitions I pretend you are him

You are clearly a figment of my imagination

This lesson I knew but never sank in

A physical mirror of ego and indecision

no blinking

are you talking to me or am I speaking

              open eyes

time for applying lessons Practically

depress the button

with one click

eyes focus beyond the blurriness

Look towards the horizon

He's gone

     Rays converge into the sun

And I see again what has always been

my true reflection

Expectations

Expectations lift

Expectations ain't shit

Wait on expectations

He'll nah

suck a dick

Expectations get nagaz in trouble

Expecting nagaz to pay back what nagaz

borrow

Families expect us to go to churches that is

hollow

Or careers they select

When they lacking basic-knowledge

Foreign rituals and rites they follow

No questions from whom

& why they were borrowed

Unanswered questions keep ignorant

mind slaves

Blinded to da truth

But wanna guide you anyway

Contradictions piling up

& they can't see

How one man's truth

Become a next mans reality

They circumcise baby boys
At a specific age
For health and rites of passage they say
African tribes are chastised repeatedly

Cause cutting a baby
Not a teen
Somehow decreases cruelty
Contradictions leading
Check da scenes
Who's ritual who's ceremony
Thanksgiving got immigrants
Acting out 13 colonies
Slicing up turkey to exhibit family unity
One day only

Don't mix up your place

Expecting family year round

He'll nah that's a waste

Theatrics

Actors and actress

Playing American dreams

Ain't know it's built on circus themes

Neck tie

Ain't know it's a sling

Adopting ideologies

Without reading in-between

That's what your god said don't do

Member you claimed dat's the truth

Now you forgot misleading da youths

I digress

Turkey slaughtering allocated for specific
days
Santeria slaughter chickens for Babaluwaye
Santa got his claws up in your kiddie's brain
Historic personalities we conjure up with
names
Present at the council of Nicene that day
Deciding which books to delete
& which to save
Modern rituals fed on foreign doctrines
Spirits sick
Expectations got people all caught up in da
mix
Expectations running up tabs on what nagaz
willing to pay

Might as well be a slave betrayed

Tryna keep nagaz in chains

Pointing out roads

Heading you straight to graves

With age

you supposed to gain grace

but they caught in the rat race perpetuating

hate

Expect you to fall when you wanna stand

firm

instead of tryna lift us up they watch & screw

with heart burn

Bitter that they neva had the balls

Bitter that we can truly have it all

Bitter that we connected to the streets

Bitter we communicate betta then they

narrow minds can conceive

Bitter that the bitterness they taste

ain't sweet

So fuck it

Fuck dem

& fuck what they think

Expectations take you for a ride

When chicks expect this naga

to be like the last guy

Expectations keep you searching for shit that

ain't there

Reaching out for nagaz who ain't really care

Intangible fantasies

How you think it should be

Expectations in relationships
fuck shit up wholly
All of a sudden she a bitch if she
suck his dick thoroughly
Expectations climax when he up
for the panties
Expectations keep nagaz twisted
Taking blue-movies for reality
Reenacting scenes mentally
Sub-conscious imagery
that seeps out selectively
Expectations screwing with nagaz heads
Expectations got nagaz mixing up
Fuckas for Friends
When it seems they closing in on the bend

Expectations crash and reality sets in

Pussy bets under his estimates

Conversation lessens

Revelations increase

Expecting you to bow to his expectations

Beneath-sheets

like that's all you worth

no brains are under-skirts

just intentions that lurk

below radar lasers beaming

Snipers shoot first then they listen

focused in one direction

pussy targets

can't reason

Nagaz go deaf when they dick get to steaming

Pouting 2 begging

Mad he ain't won

Expectations turn these nagaz into my sonz

And he see his position is only getting worse

And you see

when I spit my lyrics reverse

Like when we walk

I keep my pace first

thoughts & concepts jump ahead &

backwards

picking up things on its journey with words

Living beyond the pen

skipping through fields

different dimensions

From stars to love

Biology to dreaming
From discovering new galaxy's
to modern cap-ital-list thinking
Mur-da-rah vocabulary we teach
You see with expectations you never know
where you reach

Also another phenomenon I saw in regard to the lightnings; how some of the stars arise and become lightnings and cannot part with their new form.

Chapter 44, *The Lost Book Of Enoch*

_____

Glossary

enochisms; *the humming's of the cosmos*

leleet; *dawn (modern Ethiopic)*

gen; *but (modern Ethiopic)*

Geez; *ecclesiastic language that evolved out of Abyssinia dating back as early as the 9ᵗʰ century B.C*

Abyssinia; *ancient empire of modern day Ethiopia*

ras; *head, self, my own (modern Ethiopic)* **also** *rank in Abyssinian imperial court* **equivalent to** *that of duke*

dejazmach; *rank in the Abyssinian imperial court* **equivalent to** *commander or count*

nagaz; used ambiguously here: *lost kingz, etymology* nagas *priest class of the mother goddess in ancient Africa* note: ***negus;*** *(modern Ethiopic) Abyssinian king, lord, glory, black and god* respectively

hu; *personification of divine utterance in ancient Egypt, 2nd letter in Ethiopic alphabet* also *masculine, fire*

sa; *personification of divine knowledge/ omniscience feminine, water* also *46ᵗʰ letter in the Ethiopic alphabet*

council of nicene (nicea); *first ecumenical council 325 AD Nicea, modern day Iznik, Turkey*

What does *Lebeyt* mean though?

Lebeyt was taken from the root of her name pronounced Bey-te-le—heym. When you drop "heym" and shift "le" to the front you are left with what translates to *the house*.

We are the house as women aren't we? Lebeyt questions; *We house creation within our wombs. It isn't until a woman touches the house that it truly becomes a home. We are more than a house though. We are the temple. The body is a temple. We must respect it as so. We must remove our shoes before entering and sweep out its corners, for to receive you must release.* She explains.

LeBeyt etymology

The name *Lebeyt* derives from the root of the author's first name pronounced *Bey-te-le-heym*

Beyt translates to "the House" in regional Semitic languages

Beyt-el is first mentioned in the book Genesis (28:19)

El translates Elohim in regional Semitic languages denoting the creator.

El turns to *Le* in Ge'ez and Ethiopic idioms

Note: *el* or *il* in Latin semantics often denote the *masculine* or *ambiguous plural preposition*

Fig. 1

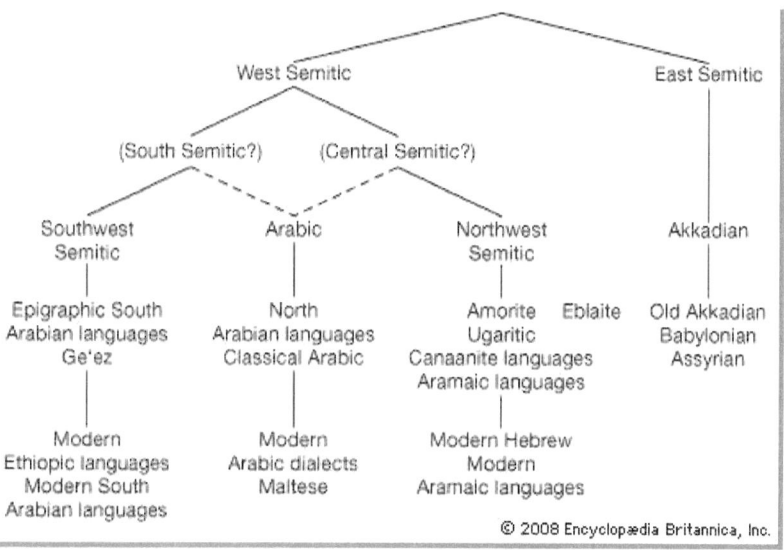

© 2008 Encyclopædia Britannica, Inc.

Figure 1:

Relationship between to Semitic languages. Adapted from "Semitic languages," by David Testen, 2015, Encyclopedia Britannica. Retrieved March 1, 2017, from https://www.britannica.com/topic/Semitic-languages Copyright 2008 by Encyclopedia Britannica, inc.

More from DHUbooks

HIGHle Qal a collaboration of
lyric prose
Lebeyt Seifu-Mikael
BGZ Teffera

Dancehall University presents
Andromeda a novel
Lebeyt Seifu-Mikael

YeAwuqt Mesaf (Book of
Knowledge)
Saif al Jabbar

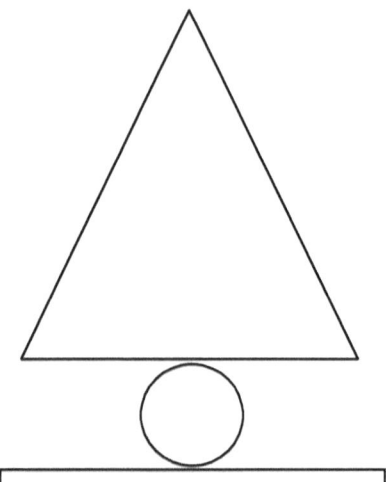

www.ingramcontent.com/pod-product-compliance
Lightning Source LLC
Chambersburg PA
CBHW020607110726

47899CB00002B/411